Dr. Seuss's
Book of
Bedtime Stories

Dr. Seuss's Book of Bedtime Stories

CONTENTS

Collins

An imprint of HarperCollinsPublishers

An omnibus edition adapted from *Dr. Seuss's Sleep Book,*
Thidwick the Big-Hearted Moose and *Horton Hears a Who!* First
published in hardback in the UK 1998 by HarperCollins*Children's*
Books, a Division of HarperCollins*Publishers* Ltd., 77-85 Fulham
Palace Road, London W6 8JB. This paperback edition
published in the UK 2002.

Visit our website at:
www.harpercollinschildrensbooks.co.uk

6 8 10 9 7 5

ISBN 0 00 714192 0

Dr. Seuss's Sleep Book © 1962, 1990 by
Dr. Seuss Enterprises L.P. All rights reserved
First published by Random House Inc., New York, USA
First published in the UK 1964
Thidwick the Big-Hearted Moose © 1948, 1975 by
Dr. Seuss Enterprises L.P. All rights reserved
First published by Random House Inc., New York, USA
First published in the UK 1968
Horton Hears a Who! © 1954, 1982 by
Dr. Seuss Enterprises L.P. All rights reserved
First published by Random House Inc., New York, USA
First published in the UK 1976

Printed and bound in Hong Kong

For Marie and Bert Hupp

The news
Just came in
From the County of Keck
That a very small bug
By the name of Van Vleck
Is yawning so wide
You can look down his neck.

This may not seem
Very important, I know.
But it *is*. So I'm bothering
Telling you so.

A yawn is quite catching, you see. Like a cough.
It just takes one yawn to start other yawns off.
NOW the news has come in that some friends of Van Vleck's
Are yawning so wide you can look down *their* necks.

At this moment, right now,
Under seven more noses,
Great yawns are in blossom.
They're blooming like roses.

The yawn of that one little bug is still spreading!
According to latest reports, it is heading
Across the wide fields, through the sleepy night air,
Across the whole country toward every-which-where.
And people are gradually starting to say,
"I feel rather drowsy. I've had quite a day."

Creatures are starting to think about rest.
Two Biffer-Baum Birds are now building their nest.
They do it each night. And quite often I wonder
How they do this big job without making a blunder.
But that is *their* problem.
Not yours. And not mine.
The point is: They're going to bed.
And that's fine.

Sleep thoughts
Are spreading
Throughout the whole land.
The time for night-brushing of teeth is at hand.
Up at Herk-Heimer Falls, where the great river rushes
And crashes down crags in great gargling gushes,
The Herk-Heimer Sisters are using their brushes.
Those falls are just grand for tooth-brushing beneath
If you happen to be up that way with your teeth.

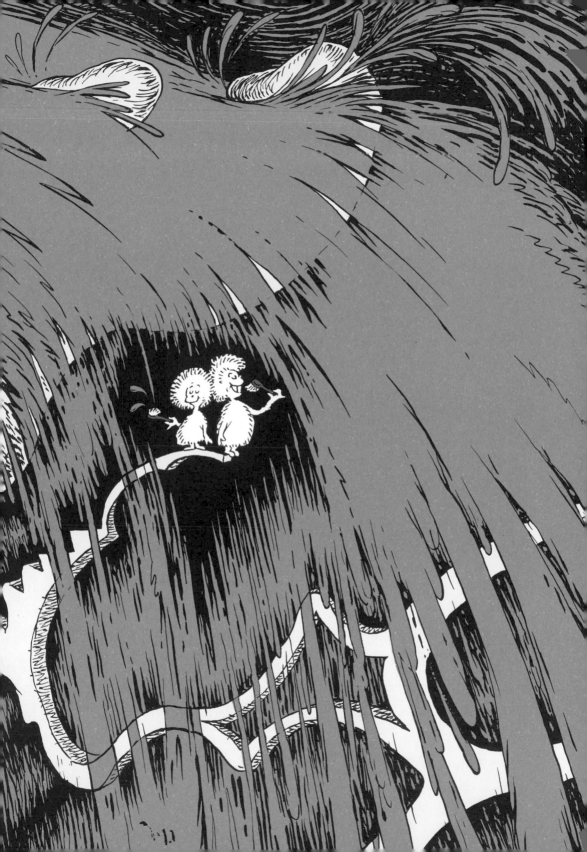

The news just came in from the Castle of Krupp
That the lights are all out and the drawbridge is up.
And the old drawbridge draw-er just said with a yawn,
"My drawbridge is drawn and it's going to stay drawn
'Til the milkman delivers the milk, about dawn.
I'm going to bed now. So nobody better
Come round with a special delivery letter."

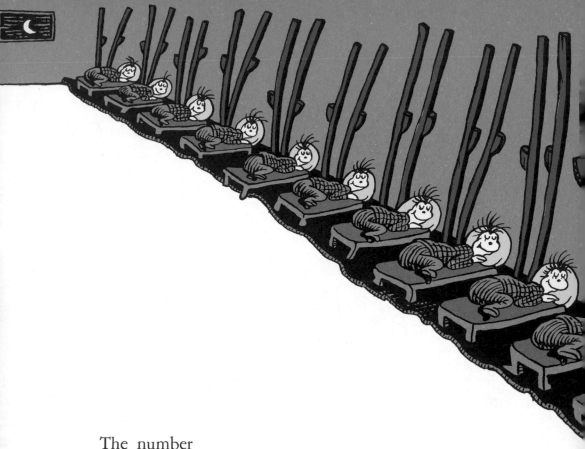

The number
Of sleepers
Is steadily growing.
Bed is where
More and more people are going.
In Culpepper Springs, in the Stilt-Walkers' Hall,
The stilt-walkers' stilts are all stacked on the wall.
The stilt-walker walkers have called it a day.
They're all tuckered out and they're snoozing away.
This is very big news. It's important to know.
And that's why I'm bothering telling you so.

Way out in the west, in the town of Mercedd,
The Hinkle-Horn Honking Club just went to bed.
Every horn has been quietly hung on a hook,
For the night, in its own private Hinkle-Horn Nook.

All this long, happy day, they've been honking about
And the Hinkle-Horn Honkers have honked themselves out.
But they'll wake up quite fresh in the morning. And then...
They'll all start Hinkle-Horn honking again.

Everywhere, creatures
Are falling asleep.
The Collapsible Frink
Just collapsed in a heap.
And, by adding the Frink
To the others before,
I am able to give you
The Who's-Asleep-Score:
Right now, forty thousand
Four hundred and four
Creatures are happily,
Deeply in slumber.
I think you'll agree
That's a whopping fine number.

Counting up sleepers..?
Just how do we do it..?
Really quite simple. There's nothing much to it.
We find out how many, we learn the amount
By an Audio-Telly-o-Tally-o Count.
On a mountain, halfway between Reno and Rome,
We have a machine in a plexiglass dome
Which listens and looks into everyone's home.
And whenever it sees a new sleeper go flop,
It jiggles and lets a new Biggel-Ball drop.
Our chap counts these balls as they plup in a cup.
And that's how we know who is down and who's up.

KEEP OUT

Do you talk in your sleep . . ?
It's a wonderful sport
And I have some news of this sport to report.
The World-Champion Sleep-Talkers, Jo and Mo Redd-Zoff,
Have just gone to sleep and they're talking their heads off.
For fifty-five years, now, each chattering brother
Has babbled and gabbled all night to the other.

They've talked about laws and they've talked about gauze.
They've talked about paws and they've talked about flaws.
They've talked quite a lot about old Santa Claus.
And the reason I'm telling you this is because
You should take up this sport. It's just fine for the jaws.

Do you walk in your sleep . . ?
I just had a report
Of some interesting news of this popular sport.
Near Finnigan Fen, there's a sleepwalking group
Which not only walks, but it walks a-la-hoop!
Every night they go miles. Why, they walk to such length
They have to keep eating to keep up their strength.

So, every so often, one puts down his hoop,
Stops hooping and does some quick snooping for soup.
That's why they are known as the Hoop-Soup-Snoop Group.

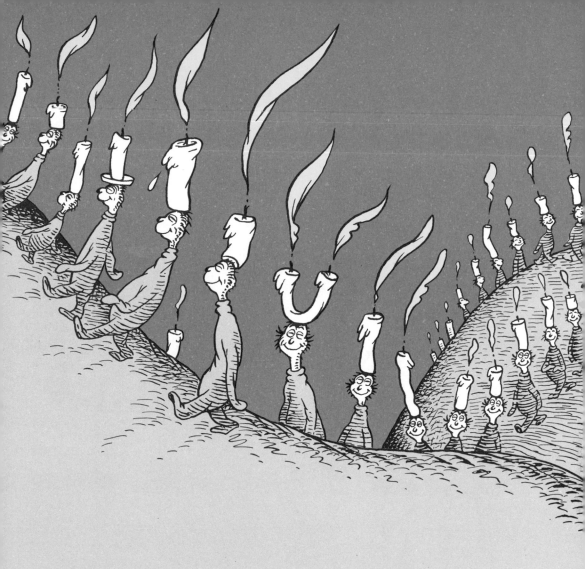

Sleepwalking, too, are the Curious Crandalls
Who sleepwalk on hills with assorted-sized candles.
The Crandalls walk nightly in slumbering peace
In spite of slight burns from the hot dripping grease.
The Crandalls wear candles because they walk far
And, if they wake up,
Want to see where they are.

Now the news has arrived
From the Valley of Vail
That a Chippendale Mupp has just bitten his tail,
Which he does every night before shutting his eyes.
Such nipping sounds silly. But, really, it's wise.

He has no alarm clock. So this is the way
He makes sure that he'll wake at the right time of day.
His tail is so long, he won't feel any pain
'Til the nip makes the trip and gets up to his brain.
In exactly eight hours, the Chippendale Mupp
Will, at last, feel the bite and yell "Ouch!" and wake up.

A Mr. and Mrs. J. Carmichael Krox
Have just gone to bed near the town of Fort Knox.
And they, by the way, have the finest of clocks.

I'm not at all sure that I quite quite understand
Just how the thing works, with that one extra hand.
But I *do* know this clock does one very slick trick.
It doesn't tick tock. How it goes, is tock tick.
So, with ticks in its tocker, and tocks in its ticker
It saves lots of time and the sleepers sleep quicker.

What a fine night for sleeping! From all that I hear,
It's the best night for sleeping in many a year.
They're even asleep in the Zwieback Motel!
And people don't usually sleep there too well.

The beds are like rocks and, as everyone knows,
The sheets are too short. They won't cover your toes.
SO, if people are actually sleeping in THERE...
It's a great night for sleeping! It must be the air.

It's a great night for snores! I just had a report
Of some boys who are tops in this musical sport.
The snortiest snorers in all our fair land
Are Snorter McPhail and his Snore-a-Snort Band.
This band can snore *Dixie* and old *Swanee River*
So loud it would make forty elephants shiver.

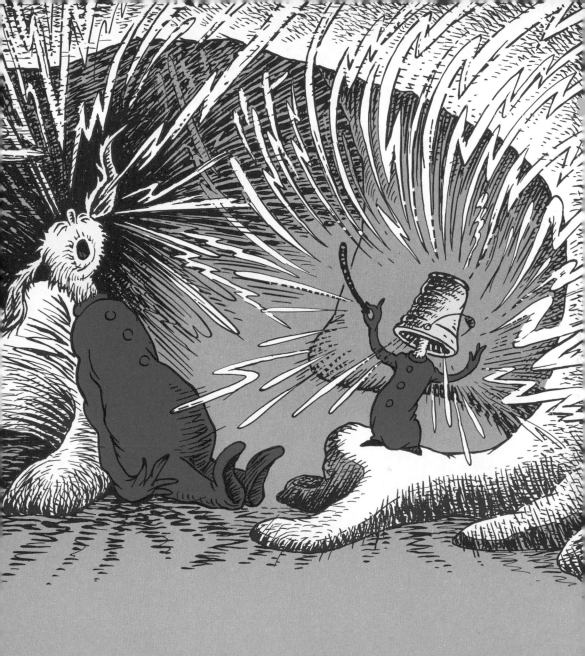

The loudest of all of the boys is McPhail.
HE snores with his head in a three-gallon pail.
So they snore in a cave twenty miles out of town.
If they snored closer in, they would snore the town down.

Do you know who's asleep
Out in Foona-Lagoona..?
Two very nice
Foona-Lagoona Baboona.

We've added them into our Who's-Asleep Count
Which has grown to a really amazing amount.
Exactly eight million, eight hundred and eight
Creatures are sleeping now! Isn't that great!

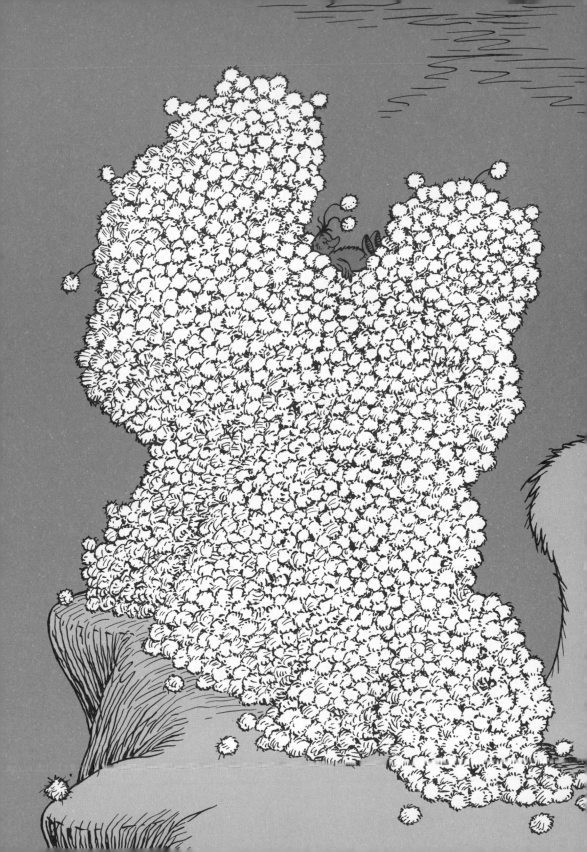

A Jedd is in bed,
And the bed of a Jedd
Is the softest
Of beds in the world,
It is said.
He makes it from pom poms
He grows on his head.
And he's sleeping right now
On the softest of fluff,
Completely exhausted
From growing the stuff.

The news has come in from the District of Dofft
That two Offt are asleep and they're sleeping aloft.
And how are they able to sleep off the ground..?
I'll tell you. I weighed one last week and I found
That an Offt is SO light he weighs minus one pound!

A moose is asleep.

He is dreaming of moose drinks.

A goose is asleep.

He is dreaming of goose drinks.

That's well and good when a moose dreams of moose juice.

And nothing goes wrong when a goose dreams of goose juice.

But it isn't too good when a moose and a goose
Start dreaming they're drinking the other one's juice.
Moose juice, not goose juice, is juice for a moose
And goose juice, not moose juice, is juice for a goose.
So, when goose gets a mouthful of juices of moose's
And moose gets a mouthful of juices of goose's,
They always fall out of their beds screaming screams.
SO . . .
I'm warning you, now! Never drink in your dreams.

Speaking of dreaming,
I think you should note
That the Bumble-Tub Club Is now dreaming afloat.
Every night they go dreaming down Bumble-Tub Creek
Except for one night, every third or fourth week,
When they stop for repairs. 'Cause their bumble-tubs leak.
But tonight they're afloat, full of dreams, full of bliss,
And that's why I'm bothering telling you this.

At the fork of a road
In the Vale of Va-Vode
Five foot-weary salesmen have laid down their load.
All day they've raced round in the heat, at top speeds,
Unsuccessfully trying to sell Zizzer-Zoof Seeds
Which nobody wants because nobody needs.

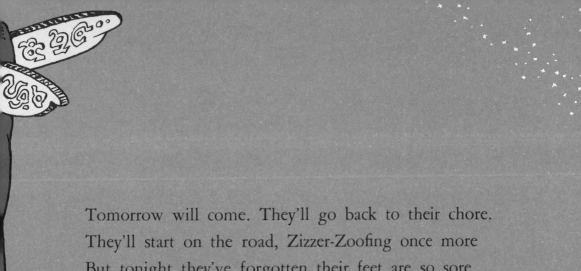

Tomorrow will come. They'll go back to their chore.
They'll start on the road, Zizzer-Zoofing once more
But tonight they've forgotten their feet are so sore.
And that's what the wonderful night time is for.

Everywhere,
Creatures
Have shut off their voices.
They've all gone to bed
In the beds of their choices.

They're sleeping in nooks. And they're sleeping in cracks.
Some on their tummies, and some on their backs.
They're peacefully sleeping in comfortable holes.
Some, even, on soft-tufted barber shop poles.
The number of sleepers is now past the millions!
The number of sleepers is now in the billions!

They're sleeping on steps! And on strings! And on floors!
In mailboxes, ships, and the keyholes of doors!
Every worm on a fishhook is safe for the night.
Every fish in the sea is too sleepy to bite.
Every whale in the ocean has turned off his spout.
Every light between here and Far Foodle is out.
And now, adding things up, we are way beyond billions!
Our Who's-Asleep-Score is now up in the Zillions!

Ninety-nine zillion,
Nine trillion and two
Creatures are sleeping!
So . . .
How about you?

When you put out *your* light,
Then the number will be
Ninety-nine zillion
Nine trillion and three.

Good night.

EXTRA MOOSE MOSS
for HELEN

THIDWICK
the Big-Hearted
MOOSE

Up at Lake Winna-Bango . . . the far northern shore . . .
Lives a huge herd of moose, about sixty or more,
And they all go around in a big happy bunch
Looking for nice tender moose-moss to munch.

Up at Lake Winna-Bango, one day, they were lunching,
Just strolling along and enjoying their munching . . .
(For the moose-moss that day was especially fine) . . .
When it happened that Thidwick, the last moose in line,
Saw a Bingle Bug sitting.
The bug called out, "Hey!
It's *such* a long road
And it's *such* a hot day,
Would you mind if I rode
On your horns for a way?"

"Of course not!" smiled Thidwick, the Big-Hearted Moose.
"I'm happy my antlers can be of some use.
There's room there to spare, and I'm happy to share!
Be my guest and I hope that you're comfortable there!"

So the Bingle Bug picked out a nice easy seat
And the moose went on looking for moose-moss to eat.

Well...
An hour or so later
The bug heard a squeak,
And he heard the small voice
Of a Tree-Spider speak.
"I say!" said the spider,
"You've got a fine place!
That moose seems quite friendly,
Has such a nice face...
If I got on, *too,*
Do you think he would mind...?"

"Hop aboard!" laughed the bug. "And I think that you'll find
That the moose won't object. He's the big-hearted kind!"

"I accept," said the spider,
"With joy and delight."
And he started a web
On the horn to the right.

While the spider was spinning, he heard a gay song
And a fresh little Zinn-a-zu Bird came along.
He stopped. And he stared. And he chirped, "Well! *Well!* WELL!
What a smart place to build! What a great place to dwell!
I've been living on *trees* ever since I was born,
But here's something *new!* Why not live on a *horn!*
If there's room there for two, then there's room there for three!"

"There's plenty of room!"
Laughed the bug. "And it's free!"

Thidwick stopped walking.

What *was* all that talking?

These guests had caught Thidwick the Moose unawares.

"Hey!" he called out. *"What goes on there upstairs?"*

"Just building a nest, sir," the Zinn-a-zu said,
And began yanking hairs out of poor Thidwick's head.
And he plucked out exactly two hundred and four!
"Don't worry," he laughed. "You can always grow more!"

Then he dozed off to sleep in his fine moose-hair nest.
"This bird," murmured Thidwick, "is sort of a pest!
But I'm a good sport, so I'll just let him rest,
For a host, above all, must be nice to his guest."

"Besides, now, it's getting quite late in the day
And *surely* tomorrow they'll all go away."

But, alas! The next morning
The sun's early light
Brought to Thidwick's sad eyes
A most *un*welcome sight....

"Meet my wife!" said the bird.
"I was married last night.

"And, perhaps; by the way,
I should mention to you
That her uncle is coming
To live with us, too.
You're a very fine host
So I knew you'd be willing . . ."

Then the Uncle, a Woodpecker,
Started in drilling!

All Thidwick's friends shouted, "GET RID OF THOSE PESTS!"
"I would, but I can't," sobbed poor Thidwick. *"They're guests!"*

"Guests indeed!" his friends answered, and all of them frowned.
"If *those* are your guests, we don't want *you* around!
You can't stay with us, 'cause you're just not our sort!"
And they all turned their backs and walked off with a snort.

Now the big friendless moose walked alone and forlorn,
With four great big woodpecker holes in his horn.

"What holes!" whispered Herman, a squirrel, who spied 'em.
"What holes to hide nuts in! *Hmmm!* Mind if I tried 'em?"

"They're yours!" called the woodpecker. "Get right inside 'em!
This big-hearted moose runs a public hotel!
Bring your nuts! Bring your wife! Bring your children as well!"

So the whole squirrel family all jumped on, pell mell.

And the very next thing the poor animal knew,
A Bobcat and Turtle were living there, too!
NOW what was the big-hearted moose going to do?

Well, what would YOU do
If it happened to YOU?

You couldn't say "Skat!" 'cause that wouldn't be right.
You couldn't shout "Scram!" 'cause that isn't polite.
A host has to put up with all kinds of pests,
For a host, above all, must be nice to his guests.
So you'd try hard to smile, and you'd try to look sweet
And you'd go right on looking for moose-moss to eat.

But now it was winter and *that* wasn't easy,
For moose-moss gets scarce when the weather gets freezy.
The food was soon gone on the cold northern shore
Of Lake Winna-Bango. There just was no more!
And all Thidwick's friends swam away in a bunch
To the south of the lake where there's moose-moss to munch.

He watched the herd leaving. And then Thidwick knew
He'd starve if he stayed here! He'd have to go, too!

He stepped in the water. Then, oh! what a fuss!
"STOP!" screamed his guests. "You can't do this to us!
These horns are our home and you've no right to take
Our home to the far distant side of the lake!"

"Be fair!" Thidwick begged, with a lump in his throat. . . .

"We're fair," said the bug.
"We'll decide this by vote.
All those in favour of going, say 'AYE,'
All those in favour of staying, say 'NAY'."

"AYE!" shouted Thidwick,
But when he was done . . .

"NAY!" they all yelled.
He lost 'leven to one.

"We win!" screamed the guests, "by a very large score!"
And poor, starving Thidwick climbed back on the shore.
Then, do you know what those pests did?
They asked in some more!

They asked in a fox, who jumped in from the trees,
They asked in some mice and they asked in some fleas.
They asked a big bear in and then, if you please,
Came a swarm of three hundred and sixty-two bees!

Poor Thidwick sank down, with a groan, to his knees.
And *then*, THEN came something that made his heart freeze.

Bullets came zinging right past Thidwick's face!
Guns were bang-binging all over the place!

"Get that moose!
Get that moose!"
Thidwick heard a voice call.
"Fire again and again
And shoot straight, one and all!
We *must* get his head
For the Harvard Club wall!"

Thidwick took to his heels with that load on his head!
With five hundred pounds on his horns, the moose fled!
He could have run faster without all those pests,
But a host, above all, must be nice to his guests.

Up canyon! Off cliff! Over wild rocky trail!
With bullets bang-bouncing around him like hail!
Up gully! Through gulch! And down slippery sluice,
With his hard-hearted guests raced the soft-hearted moose!

Then finally they had him!

Because of those pests, he had run out of luck,
Because of those guests on his horns, he was stuck!

He gasped! He felt faint! And the whole world grew fuzzy!
Thidwick was finished, completely. . . .

. . . *or WAS he* . . .?

Finished . . . ?
Not Thidwick!
DECIDEDLY NOT!
It's true, he was in a most terrible spot,
But NOW he remembered a thing he'd forgot!
A wonderful something that happens each year
To the horns of all moose and the horns of all deer.

Today was the day,
Thidwick happened to know . . .

. . . that OLD horns come off so that NEW ones can grow!

And he called to the pests on his horns as he threw 'em,
"You wanted my horns; now you're quite welcome to 'em!
Keep 'em! They're yours!
As for ME, I shall take
Myself to the far distant
Side of the lake!"

And he swam Winna-Bango and found his old bunch,
And arrived just in time for a wonderful lunch
At the south of the lake, where there's moose-moss to munch.

His *old* horns today are
Where *you* knew they *would* be.
His guests are still on them,
All stuffed, as they *should* be.

For My Great Friend,
Mitsugi Nakamura
of Kyoto,
Japan.

HORTON
HEARS
A
WHO!

On the fifteenth of May, in the Jungle of Nool,
In the heat of the day, in the cool of the pool,
He was splashing...enjoying the jungle's great joys...
When Horton the elephant heard a small noise.

So Horton stopped splashing. He looked towards the sound.
"That's funny," thought Horton. "There's no one around."
Then he heard it again! Just a very faint yelp
As if some tiny person were calling for help.
"I'll help you," said Horton. "But *who* are you? *Where?*"
He looked and he looked. He could see nothing there
But a small speck of dust blowing past through the air.

"I say!" murmured Horton. "I've never heard tell
Of a small speck of dust that is able to yell.
So you know what I think? . . . Why, I think that there must
Be someone on top of that small speck of dust!
Some sort of a creature of *very* small size,
Too small to be seen by an elephant's eyes. . .

"... some poor little person who's shaking with fear
That he'll blow in the pool! He has no way to steer!
I'll just have to save him. Because, after all,
A person's a person, no matter how small."

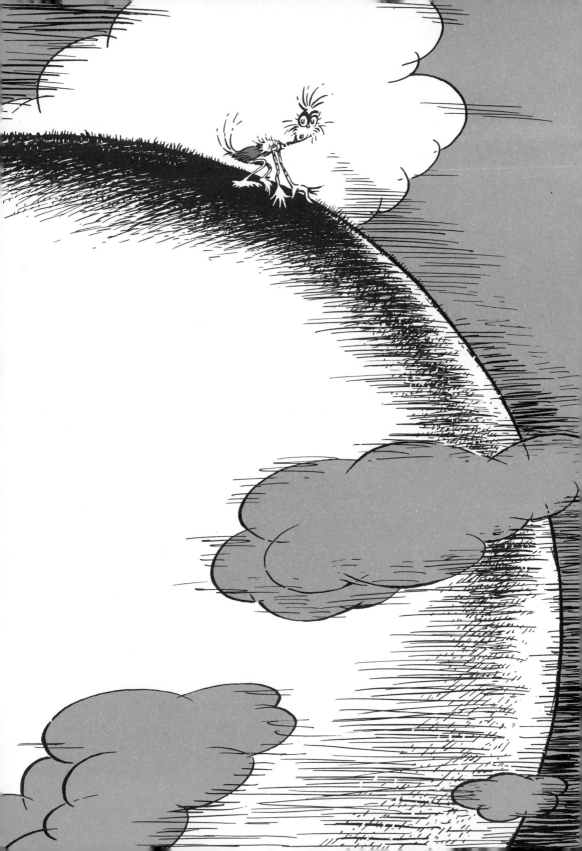

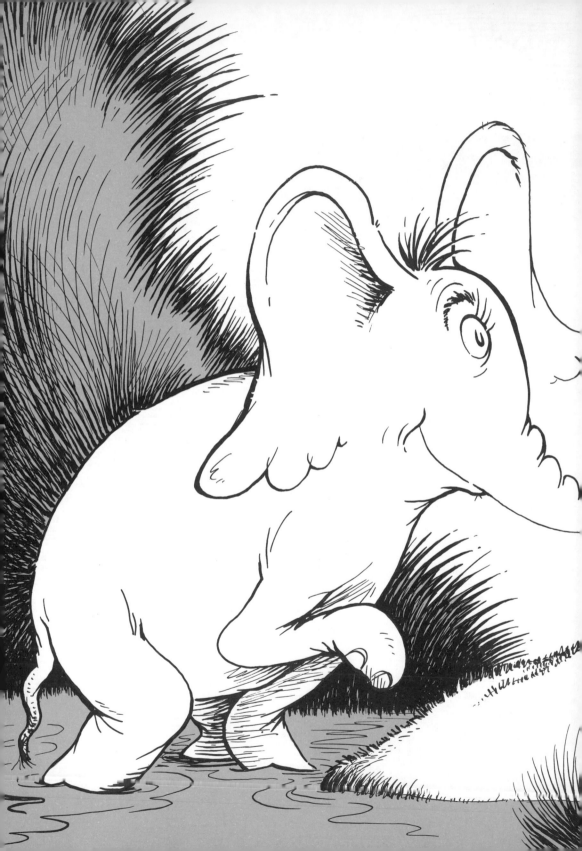

So, gently, and using the greatest of care,
The elephant stretched his great trunk through the air,
And he lifted the dust speck and carried it over
And placed it down, safe, on a very soft clover.

"Humpf!" humpfed a voice. 'Twas a sour kangaroo.
And the young kangaroo in her pouch said "Humpf!" too.
"Why, that speck is as small as the head of a pin.
A person on *that?* . . . Why, there never has been!"

"Believe me," said Horton. "I tell you sincerely,
My ears are quite keen and I heard him quite clearly.
I *know* there's a person down there. And, what's more,
Quite likely there's two. Even three. Even four.
Quite likely . . .

". . . a family, for all that we know!
A family with children just starting to grow.
So, please," Horton said, "as a favour to me,
Try not to disturb them. Just please let them be."

"I think you're a fool!" laughed the sour kangaroo
And the young kangaroo in her pouch said, "Me, too!
You're the biggest blame fool in the Jungle of Nool!"
And the kangaroos plunged in the cool of the pool.
"What terrible splashing!" the elephant frowned.
"I can't let my very small persons get drowned!
I've *got* to protect them. I'm bigger than they."
So he plucked up the clover and hustled away.

Through the high jungle tree tops, the news quickly spread:
"He talks to a dust speck! He's out of his head!
Just look at him walk with that speck on that flower!"
And Horton walked, worrying, almost an hour.
"Should I put this speck down?..." Horton thought with alarm.
"If I do, these small persons may come to great harm.
I *can't* put it down. And I *won't!* After all
A person's a person. No matter how small."

Then Horton stopped walking.
The speck-voice was talking!
The voice was so faint he could just barely hear it.
"Speak *up,* please," said Horton. He put his ear near it.

"My friend," came the voice, "you're a *very* fine friend.
You've helped all us folks on this dust speck no end.
You've saved all our houses, our ceilings and floors.
You've saved all our churches and grocery stores."

"You mean . . ." Horton gasped, "you have *buildings* there, *too?*"

"Oh, yes," piped the voice. "We most certainly do. . . .
"I know," called the voice, "I'm too small to be seen
But I'm Mayor of a town that is friendly and clean.
Our buildings, to you, would seem terribly small
But to us, who aren't big, they are wonderfully tall.
My town is called *Who*-ville, for I am a *Who*
And we *Whos* are all thankful and grateful to you."

And Horton called back to the Mayor of the town,
"You're safe now. Don't worry. I won't let you down."

But, just as he spoke to the Mayor of the speck,
Three big jungle monkeys climbed up Horton's neck!
The Wickersham Brothers came shouting, "What rot!
This elephant's talking to *Whos* who are *not!*
There *aren't* any *Whos!* And they *don't* have a Mayor!
And *we're* going to stop all this nonsense! *So there!"*

They snatched Horton's clover! They carried it off
To a black-bottomed eagle named Vlad Vlad-i-koff,
A mighty strong eagle, of very swift wing,
And they said, "Will you kindly get rid of this thing?"
And, before the poor elephant even could speak,
That eagle flew off with the flower in his beak.

All that late afternoon and far into the night
That black-bottomed bird flapped his wings in fast flight,
While Horton chased after, with groans, over stones
That tattered his toenails and battered his bones,
And begged, "Please don't harm all my little folks, who
Have as much right to live as us bigger folks do!"

But far, far beyond him, that eagle kept flapping
And over his shoulder called back, "Quit your yapping.
I'll fly the night through. I'm a bird. I don't mind it.
And I'll hide this, tomorrow, where *you'll* never find it!"

And at 6:56 the next morning he did it.
It sure was a terrible place that he hid it.
He let that small clover drop somewhere inside
Of a great patch of clovers a hundred miles wide!
"Find THAT!" sneered the bird. "But I think you will fail."
And he left
With a flip
Of his black-bottomed tail.

"I'll find it!" cried Horton. "I'll find it or bust!
I SHALL find my friends on my small speck of dust!"
And clover, by clover, by clover with care
He picked up and searched them, and called, "Are you there?"
But clover, by clover, by clover he found
That the one that he sought for was just not around.
And by noon poor old Horton, more dead than alive,
Had picked, searched, and piled up, nine thousand and five.

Then, on through the afternoon, hour after hour...
Till he found them at last! On the three millionth flower!
"My friends!" cried the elephant. "Tell me! Do tell!
Are you safe? Are you sound? Are you whole? Are you well?"

From down on the speck came the voice of the Mayor:

"We've *really* had trouble! Much more than our share.
When that black-bottomed birdie let go and we dropped,
We landed so hard that our clocks have all stopped.
Our tea-pots are broken. Our rocking-chairs smashed.
And our bicycle tires all blew up when we crashed.
So, Horton, *please!*" pleaded that voice of the Mayor's,
"Will you stick by us *Whos* while we're making repairs?"

"Of course," Horton answered. "Of course I will stick.
I'll stick by you small folks through thin and through thick!"

"Humpf!"
Humpfed a voice!
"For almost two days you've run wild and insisted
On chatting with persons who've never existed.
Such carryings-on in our peaceable jungle!
We've had quite enough of your bellowing bungle!
And I'm here to state," snapped the big kangaroo,
"That your silly nonsensical game is all through!"
And the young kangaroo in her pouch said, "Me, too!"

"With the help of the Wickersham Brothers and dozens
Of Wickersham Uncles and Wickersham Cousins
And Wickersham In-Laws, whose help I've engaged,
You're going to be roped! And you're going to be caged!
And, as for your dust speck ... *hah*! *That* we shall boil
In a hot steaming kettle of Beezle-Nut oil!"

"*Boil* it? ..." gasped Horton!
"Oh, that you *can't* do!
It's all full of persons!
They'll *prove* it to you!"

"Mr. Mayor! Mr. Mayor!" Horton called. "Mr. Mayor!
You've *got* to prove now that you really are there!
So call a big meeting. Get everyone out.
Make every *Who* holler! Make every *Who* shout!
Make every *Who* scream! If you don't, every *Who*
Is going to end up in a Beezle-Nut stew!"

And, down on the dust speck, the scared little Mayor
Quick called a big meeting in *Who*-ville Town Square.
And his people cried loudly. They cried out in fear:
"We are here! We are here! We are here! We are here!"

The elephant smiled: "That was clear as a bell.
You kangaroos surely heard *that* very well."
"All I heard," snapped the big kangaroo, "was the breeze,
And the faint sound of wind through the far-distant trees.
I heard no small voices. And you didn't either."
And the young kangaroo in her pouch said, "Me, neither."

"Grab him!" they shouted. "And cage the big dope!
Lasso his stomach with ten miles of rope!
Tie the knots tight so he'll *never* shake loose!
Then dunk that dumb speck in the Beezle-Nut juice!"

Horton fought back with great vigour and vim
But the Wickersham gang was too many for him.
They beat him! They mauled him! They started to haul
Him into his cage! But he managed to call
To the Mayor: "Don't give up! I believe in you all!
A person's a person, no matter how small!
And you very small persons will *not* have to die
If you make yourselves heard! *So come on, now, and TRY!*"

The Mayor grabbed a tom-tom. He started to smack it.
And, all over *Who*-ville, they whooped up a racket.
They rattled tin kettles! They beat on brass pans,
On garbage pail tops and old cranberry cans!
They blew on bazookas and blasted great toots
On clarinets, oom-pahs and boom-pahs and flutes!

Great gusts of loud racket rang high through the air.
They rattled and shook the whole sky! And the Mayor
Called up through the howling mad hullabaloo:
"Hey, Horton! *How's this?* Is our sound coming through?"

And Horton called back, "I can hear you just fine.
But the kangaroos' ears aren't as strong, quite, as mine.
They don't hear a thing! Are you *sure* all your boys
Are doing their best? Are they ALL making noise?
Are you sure every *Who* down in *Who*-ville is working?
Quick! Look through your town! Is there anyone shirking?"

Through the town rushed the Mayor, from the east to the west.
But *every*one seemed to be doing his best.
*Every*one seemed to be yapping or yipping!
*Every*one seemed to be beeping or bipping!
But it *wasn't enough,* all this ruckus and roar!
He HAD to find someone to help him make more.
He raced through each building! He searched floor-to-floor!

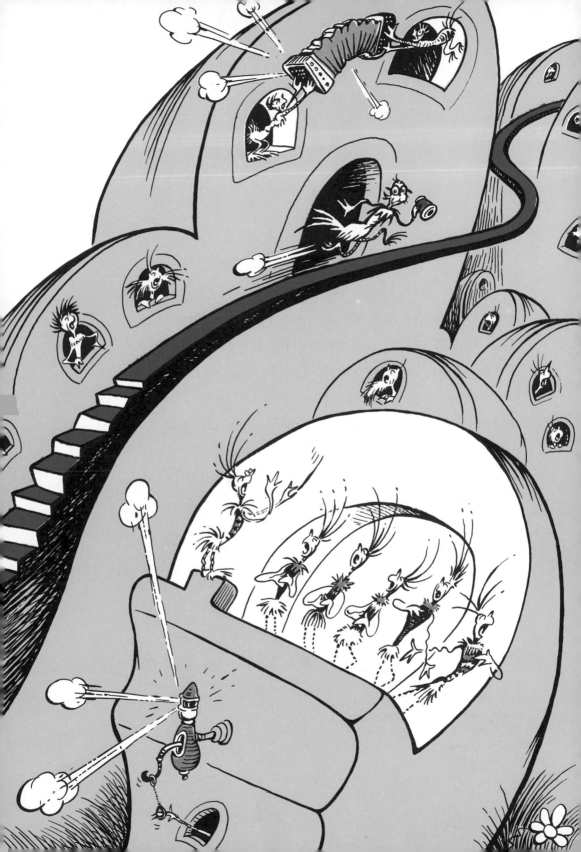

And, just as he felt he was getting nowhere,
And almost about to give up in despair,
He suddenly burst through a door and that Mayor
Discovered one shirker! Quite hidden away
In the Fairfax Apartments (Apartment 12-J)
A very small, *very* small shirker named Jo-Jo
Was standing, just standing, and bouncing a Yo-Yo!
Not making a sound! Not a yipp! Not a chirp!
And the Mayor rushed inside and he grabbed the young twerp!

And he climbed with the lad up the Eiffelberg Tower.

"This," cried the Mayor, "is your town's darkest hour!
The time for all *Whos* who have blood that is red
To come to the aid of their country!" he said.
"We've GOT to make noises in greater amounts!
So, open your mouth, lad! For every voice counts!"

Thus he spoke as he climbed. When they got to the top,
The lad cleared his throat and he shouted out, "YOPP!"

And that Yopp . . .
That one small, extra Yopp put it over!
Finally, at last! From that speck on that clover
Their voices were heard! They rang out clear and clean.
And the elephant smiled. "Do you see what I mean? . . .
They've proved they ARE persons, no matter how small.
And their whole world was saved by the Smallest of All!"

"How true! Yes, how true," said the big kangaroo.
"And, from now on, you know what I'm planning to do? . . .
From now on, I'm going to protect them with you!"
And the young kangaroo in her pouch said, . . .

"... ME, TOO!
From sun in the summer. From rain when it's fall-ish,
I'm going to protect them. No matter how small-ish!"

Dr.Seuss™

The more that you **read**,
the more things **you** will know.
The more that you **learn**,
the **more** places you'll go!
– I Can Read With My Eyes Shut!

With over **30 paperbacks to collect** there's a book for all ages and reading abilities, and now there's never been a better time to have **fun** with **Dr.Seuss!**
Simply collect 5 tokens from the back of each Dr.Seuss book and send in for your

FREE Dr.Seuss poster
(rrp £3.99)

Send your 5 tokens and a completed voucher to:
Dr. Seuss poster offer, PO Box 142, Horsham, UK, RH13 5FJ (UK residents only)

Title: Mr ☐   Mrs ☐   Miss ☐   Ms ☐

First Name:_____   Surname:_____

Address:_____

Post Code:_____   E-Mail Address:_____

Date of Birth:_____   Signature of parent/guardian:_____

TICK HERE IF YOU DO NOT WISH TO RECEIVE FURTHER INFORMATION ABOUT CHILDREN'S BOOKS ☐

Read them **together**, read them **alone**, read them **aloud** and make **reading fun!**
With over **30 wacky stories** to choose from, now it's **easier than ever** to find the
right **Dr. Seuss** books for your child – just let the **back cover colour** guide you!

Blue back books
for sharing with your child

Dr. Seuss' ABC
The Foot Book
Hop on Pop
Mr. Brown Can Moo! Can You?
One Fish, Two Fish, Red Fish, Blue Fish
There's a Wocket in my Pocket!

Green back books
for children just beginning to read on their own

And to Think That I Saw It on Mulberry Street
The Cat in the Hat
The Cat in the Hat Comes Back
Fox in Socks
Green Eggs and Ham
I Can Read With My Eyes Shut!
I Wish That I Had Duck Feet
Marvin K. Mooney Will You Please Go Now!
Oh, Say Can You Say?
Oh, the Thinks You Can Think!
Ten Apples Up on Top
Wacky Wednesday

Yellow back books
for fluent readers to enjoy

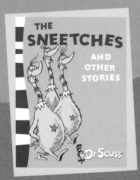

Daisy-Head Mayzie
Did I Ever Tell You How Lucky You Are?
Dr. Seuss' Sleep Book
Horton Hatches the Egg
Horton Hears a Who!
How the Grinch Stole Christmas!
If I Ran the Circus
If I Ran the Zoo
I Had Trouble in Getting to Solla Sollew
The Lorax
Oh, the Places You'll Go!
On Beyond Zebra
Scrambled Eggs Super!
The Sneetches and other stories
Thidwick the Big-Hearted Moose
Yertle the Turtle and other stories